THE POND

Antony Dawson

MAPLE
PUBLISHERS

The Pond

Author: Antony Dawson

Illustrations © Maple Publishers

Text Copyright © Antony Dawson (2022)

The right of Antony Dawson to be identified as author of this work has been asserted by the author in accordance with section 77 and 78 of the Copyright, Designs and Patents Act 1988.

First Published in 2022

ISBN 978-1-915492-44-9 (Paperback)
       978-1-915492-45-6 (E-Book)

Book Cover Design, Illustrations, and Layout by:
        Maple Publishers
        www.maplepublishers.com

Published by:
        Maple Publishers
        1 Brunel Way,
        Slough,
        SL1 1FQ, UK
        www.maplepublishers.com

Edited by:
        Alexa Dawson

Index

Summary

Rana's pond is going to be destroyed to make way for new buildings (homes for the Giant Feet). This story is the journey of Rana and his group of friends in their quest to find a safe place to live.

Chapter 1

The Pond

Rana sat very still in his favorite spot, as he did most evenings when the sun was low on the horizon. He looked out over the greens and browns of the reedmace and bulrushes that bordered the Pond. As a frog, Rana loved the Pond- it was his home. He had been born there and, although he often hopped away to explore, he never went too far. He always returned every evening to the place he was most comfortable, where he could gaze over his beloved Pond.

However, this evening was different somehow. It was just a feeling Rana had, like something had changed or was missing in the Pond. He did not know what, but something was just not quite right. It made him feel sad, which was unusual because Rana was normally a very happy little frog.

On the other side of the Pond, Mr. and Mrs. Gaster were both busy at work. Mr. Gaster was a proud stickleback whose glimmering red throat seemed to glow as he darted to-and-fro, pulling on bits of sticks and pieces of pond weed. He was trying to prepare a place for Mrs. Gaster to lay her eggs. All the while, Mrs. Gaster fussed over him, saying "No, not there, no no that will never do!"

"No, something is just not quite right," she mentioned again.

Mr. Gaster looked at his wife with his bright blue eyes and asked, "What could it be?"

Right at that moment, a giant splash came from above. Out from underneath a water lily swam Tritus, his great crested back and strong tail guiding him towards the Gasters.

"Good evening," greeted Tritus.

"Hello, Tritus."

"Are you building a nest?" Tritus asked.

"Yes," Mr. Gaster replied without stopping what he was doing.

"Oh, well- uh- are you sure that's a good idea right now?" Tritus stuttered.

Mr. Gaster immediately responded with pride, "What would a newt know about building a stickleback's nest?"

"No, no, you misunderstand, Mr. Gaster. I have just been talking to Arvi."

"Arvi?" Mr. and Mrs. Gaster questioned in unison.

"Yes, Arvi. She said that there is something happening with the Pond."

"I knew things were not quite right," said Mrs. Gaster under her breath, "I haven't felt well for some time now, and it isn't just because I'm carrying eggs, it's something more. Oh dear!"

"Yes, I know what you mean," Tritus replied, "that's what I was talking about with Arvi. She wants to hold a meeting under the old willow roots tomorrow at sun up."

"Then we shall be there." Mr. Gaster declared.

"Jolly good. See you tomorrow then," Tritus said as he swam off to find his good friend, Rana.

Tritus made his way to the place he knew he would find Rana. He, like Rana, had spent all of his life in and around the Pond, and felt a special connection to it.

"Hello, Rana," called Tritus as he approached Rana's spot.

"Well, hello Tritus, my old friend," smiled Rana.

"Have you noticed the lack of dragonflies this year?"

"Yes, and not just dragonflies; there are less worms to eat, too!"

"Mmm, worms," repeated Tritus as he licked his lips, "we all likes' worms, Rana."

"Nothing is better than a feast of worms," agreed Rana.

"Yes there is," Tritus exclaimed, "two feasts of worms!"

They both laughed joyfully.

"Worms aside, Rana, there is something not quite right with the Pond. Arvi wants to hold a meeting," said Tritus, becoming more serious.

"Oh, really? Arvi, you say? Well, she would know if something were amiss," Rana replied nervously.

"Sunrise at the old willow roots, then," said Tritus before swimming off.

Chapter 2

The Meeting

Rana made his way down through the green sedge grass and yellow iris flowers towards the old willow roots, listening to the thrush of the robin and Jenny wren singing their songs to greet the great new day as dawn broke over the Pond. He hopped over the log of a fallen tree and touched his heels together in mid-air; he was happy, as he looked forward to seeing all of his friends together.

When he arrived, nobody was to be seen on land, so he dipped his head into the water. There, Rana found Mr. and Mrs. Gaster swimming towards him.

"Hello, Rana," they both said.

"Good morning!" replied Rana as he slid the rest of his body into the water.

"Have you seen Arvi yet?" asked Mrs. Gaster.

"No, I think we are the first to arrive."

"Ah, well I'm sure she is on her way," said Mr. Gaster.

Rana swam back to the surface to squat down on one of the old willow tree's twisted roots. Gazing over the yellow flowers of the spearwort and the blue-gray tones of the forget-me-not, Rana first heard the sounds of two creatures puffing and panting before seeing them pushing and pulling a decidedly odd looking object. As they came closer he saw that the creatures were his friends Arvi and Tritus.

"Good morning," Rana greeted them.

"Hello, Rana," said Arvi, while Tritus struggled with the strange object.

"Are the Gasters here?" she continued, her long whiskers twitching.

"Oh yes, they are here, but what on earth is that?" asked Rana as he pointed to the object.

"All in good time, Rana," said Arvi, sliding effortlessly into the water as only a water vole could.

"Give me a hand with this, please, Rana?" Tritus asked.

Rana helped him roll the mysterious thing to the water's edge before they both jumped into the water to join Arvi and the Gasters.

Bufo the toad slowly made his way from his home under an old rotten log towards the willow roots. He wondered what all of this fuss was about. *A meeting? Something about the Pond? Indeed,* he thought to himself. Although he trusted Arvi and got along well with everyone who lived at the Pond, he was not looking forward to the meeting since he would much rather be on his own. As Bufo approached the meeting place, he saw Arvi sitting on a root, addressing the gathering at the water's edge.

"Hello, Bufo, glad you could make it."

"Hello, all," Bufo replied, "sorry I'm late. So what's this all about?"

"It's the Giant Feet," blurted out a very upset Mrs. Gaster, "they are going to destroy the Pond!"

"They can't do that, there must be some mistake," Bufo sat down, feeling confused.

"I'm afraid it's true," frowned Tritus.

"But, why? We have done nothing to them, we never harm them, how could we? They are so big, and we are so small."

"Because the Giant Feet, or the 'humans' as they are called, are building more homes for themselves. They are getting closer and closer to the Pond," replied Arvi.

"That's why the water tastes bitter," nodded Mrs. Gaster.

"That accounts for the lack of dragonflies," Rana pointed out.

"Less worms, too," joined in Tritus.

"That's true! There are less worms!" added Bufo.

The group all looked wearily at each other. If there was one thing that all of the creatures loved, it was eating a feast of worms.

"Now you understand why we must leave the Pond and find a new home," Arvi said softly.

Leave the Pond? Rana thought to himself, *but, where would we go?* At this point, the Gasters looked incredibly worried.

"Leaving the Pond- impossible! The rest of you creatures can make your way on land, but for myself and Mrs. Gaster it is simply out of the question," Mr. Gaster began to rant.

Arvi looked over to the foreign object she and Tritus had dragged all the way to the Pond. She motioned for everybody else to look at it with her.

"It's called a 'bottle'. It is made by the Giant Feet to carry water, and it will carry you and Mrs. Gaster."

"What about my eggs?" blurted Mrs. Gaster, holding her stomach.

"All the more reason to leave, my dear Mrs. Gaster, and fast," Arvi responded.

"But- but- Mrs. Gaster and myself, in that bottle?"

It all seemed too much to handle for a proud stickleback like Mr. Gaster. Just as Arvi prepared her reply, the ground began to shake and the surface of the water began to tremble. The creatures of the Pond all dove for cover among the pondweed, hiding as horrible, loud noises echoed through the air and the water. After a while, the noises ceased. It was then that the gathering of friends realized they would all have to leave their homes and say goodbye to the Pond, and do it very soon.

Chapter 3

The Dark Woods Part One

It was decided during the morning meeting that their journey would begin at night. Arvi had explained to the rest of the group that it would be safer to start at nighttime as she could more easily see where she was going by the light of the moon. Arvi was the only one amongst the group who actually knew where they would be heading; she was very wise, and they all trusted her. When everyone met up that evening, it was Arvi who made sure they were ready for the long and somewhat unknown journey ahead.

After much discussion, Mr. Gaster finally swallowed his pride and, with his very worried looking wife, swam into the bottle. The bottle with the Gasters inside was then hauled up the bank. They all agreed to take turns pushing, pulling, and rolling the bottle.

"Is everyone ready?" called Arvi.

As ready as we'll ever be, they all thought.

So their journey began. Arvi was leading the way while Bufo and Tritus were rolling the Gasters in their bottle with Rana bringing up the rear. All of the creatures were quiet, feeling a little afraid and deep in their own thoughts as they started to leave. With a heavy heart, Rana turned his head to look back at his beloved Pond for what would be the very last time. Silently, he said goodbye to his home and the only world he had ever known, then turned his head to look toward a very uncertain future.

Arvi led the group toward the Dark Woods: through the nettles and docks, under the ferns, and onward until they reached the giant roots of the mighty oak and ash trees. They continued farther and farther together into the unknown depths of the Dark Woods.

"What was that noise?" Rana jumped.

"It's the night creatures who live in the woods," said Bufo.

"Keep quiet and keep up," whispered Arvi, "we do not want to draw attention to ourselves in this place."

It was dark, damp, and still, with the occasional strange noise, but they met no other creatures that night. After what seemed to them like the longest time, Arvi called the group to halt at the roots of an old elm tree. She suggested that everyone should get some rest while she ran ahead to look at the next part of their journey.

"I'll be back shortly," Arvi promised, "and I will see if I can find some worms to eat." With that, she bounded off into the Dark Woods.

"How are the Gasters doing?" asked Rana.

"They are asleep," replied Tritus.

"That sounds like a good idea to me," mumbled a very tired Bufo, who then promptly crawled up next to the Gaster's bottle and fell fast asleep. Rana and Tritus felt too nervous to sleep, so they began to discuss the Giant Feet and their destructive ways.

Some distance away, Arvi jumped onto a sycamore root before climbing up the smooth, gray bark of the trunk to get to a low branch. Here she sat upright and motionless, staring silently ahead as if she was waiting for someone- or something. After a while, her small ears pricked up as she heard a faint noise above her in the treetops.

"*Ker-wick, ker-wick!*"

Then, *whoosh*! Something large flew right past Arvi and landed on a branch opposite of where she sat. It was the Night Shadow! Her large, black eyes stared deep into Arvi's. The Night Shadow was an elder tawny owl with an all-knowing wisdom similar to Arvi's. She knew all there was to know about the Dark Woods: where to go, where not to go, who to befriend, and who to avoid. The Night Shadow was also an old friend to Arvi, who had been a help and a guide in times of need.

The two sat silently for some time staring at each other. They were not speaking aloud so much as they were passing their thoughts between one another. Once their moment had passed, with the nod of her head and a wink of an eye, the Night Shadow flew off to carry on with her night vigil in the Dark Woods.

After her meeting with the Night Shadow, Arvi felt a new confidence. She naturally understood what to do and where to go next. It was now time to find her friends and lead them to safety.

"No, I can't think of anything good to say about them!" complained Tritus as he sat at the elm tree's roots.

"It's true," agreed Rana, "they are nothing but trouble, crushing and squashing everything in their path. Now they are going to destroy our lovely Pond!"

They were talking about the Giant Feet, as they called the humans, and how they could find nothing good at all about them.

"They are not all bad," said a voice from under the Gaster's bottle.

"What did you say?" asked a shocked Rana.

"They are not all bad, the Giant Feet!" repeated Bufo, looking refreshed after his sound sleep under the bottle.

"What on earth makes you say that, Bufo?" Rana inquired, still a bit shocked.

"I lived with one for a whole winter season once. He was a young Giant Foot; he fed me worms and I lived in his garden."

Rana and Tritus gave each other a look and shrugged. They both thought that Bufo was a very strange creature to be living with the Giant Feet.

"Did someone mention worms?" cried Arvi to her friends as she arrived back from her travels. "Then let's try these!"

With that, she produced a large ball of big, fat, juicy worms. Rana jumped with glee and touched his heels in the air.

"Jolly good, Arvi," said Tritus, "and just in time! I am ever so hungry."

Even Bufo looked happy at the idea of feasting on juicy worms. Arvi unscrewed the Gaster's bottle and popped some worms in just as they began to wake up.

"That will fill you up, Mr. and Mrs. Gaster. Fill up your tummies with food, everyone," Arvi told them all, "and build up your strength. We still have a long way to go before our journey is over."

After the group had eaten their fill and gotten enough rest, they began to prepare themselves for the next part of their adventure until Arvi told them it was time to go.

Chapter 4

The Dark Woods Part Two

Onward they traveled further into the Dark Woods; it was so dark, in fact, that they could not tell if it was night or day. They could, however, smell the rain before it came. And, rain it did! Pouring down from wherever the sky was, it rained for many days and nights, but none of the group complained. They all loved the rain, and preferred to be wet rather than dry.

One night, as the group was resting under some ferns at the base of a great, old oak tree, they heard a shrill cry.

"What was that?" asked Rana.

Tritus and Bufo looked at one another.

"I don't know," answered Tritus.

"Arvi would know," said Bufo as he crept further under the safety of the ferns. But, Arvi had run ahead as she did every night to check the route for the next part of their journey.

"*Ke-ke!*"

"There it is again," said Rana, "I'm going to take a look."

"No, please stay here," cried Bufo, "it will be safer if we all stick together!"

"I agree with Bufo, it is better if we stick together. We have to look after the Gasters, too," said Tritus.

"Oh, don't worry, I will not be too long. I will just take a quick look around to see!" exclaimed Rana before hopping off into the woods in the direction of the noise they heard. He had not gone too far before he heard an unnerving chattering and spitting sound coming from under some bracken. Then, in a flash, in front of Rana appeared a vicious looking creature with a long, reddish body. He had beady black eyes and sharp yellow teeth that matched the color of his throat and belly. Rana froze! He had never felt so scared in his life. The creature, a stoat, was much bigger than Rana and did not look friendly at all.

"I have been following you," spat the stoat.

"Oh, uh, really," stammered Rana as he tried to put on his bravest face, "I thought I heard you."

"Who are you, and what are you?" the stoat slyly asked.

"I'm Rana the frog," he answered.

"Wrong, wrong, wrong," said the grinning stoat, "you are my dinner!"

As quick as a flash, the stoat grabbed Rana's hind leg in his long, yellow teeth and dashed off into the ferns, dragging poor Rana behind him.

Rana did not know what was happening. He thought he must be having a very bad dream, but the pain in his leg was very real. *I've come all this way just to end up as a dinner for this nasty looking creature,* thought Rana.

Just then, Rana heard a *whoosh* and a scream. Next, he was falling through the air only to land in the ferns with a *bump!* There he quietly laid, very still, not daring to move a muscle. All he could hear now was the silence of the Dark Woods. The stoat was gone and Rana was all alone.

After waiting a while, Rana checked his leg. It was very sore, but he managed to crawl into the safety of a hollow. In pain and feeling sorry for himself as he sat alone, Rana cried himself to sleep as he thought of his friends and his beloved Pond.

By the time Arvi found Rana, he had already been awoken by a friendly hedgehog who went by the name of Erin. She had been kind to Rana after his experience, sharing her worms and telling him stories to keep his spirits up while also listening to his accounts of his travels. Arvi had met Erin a few times before, as Erin had visited the Pond in the past.

"There is a stream not far from here," said Erin, "and I think your group should go there. Rest up a bit before you continue your journey."

"That is a good idea," said Arvi, "we could all use a nice rest, especially Rana. That was a close encounter."

"Don't stay by the stream for too long, though. Rain is due soon, and when it rains hard the stream will run much faster. It will wash everything in and around it away! Head for the row of brambles at the edge of the pasture and you will either hear or smell the stream," advised Erin.

Arvi and Rana thanked Erin for her kindness and her help. They said their goodbyes and she wished them luck as they left for the group.

Arvi helped Rana as much as she could while they made their way back to Tritus, Bufo, and the Gasters. They were all so relieved to see that Rana was back safely, and not too badly hurt. The friends made a fuss over Rana, asking him to tell the story of all that had happened to him. All except Bufo, that is, who called Rana a "foolish frog". Even so, Bufo was pleased to see that Rana was alright.

Arvi asked for everyone's attention before telling them all about their meeting with Erin and the plans to find the stream. The news about the stream made everyone feel a new sense of excitement, especially the Gasters.

Chapter 5

The Stream

As the group of friends made their way over a large pasture towards the row of brambles, Rana told Arvi a story that Erin had told him about a hedgehog who's very life had been saved by a Giant Foot.

"Unbelievable," said Arvi, "but quite possible."

Tritus was the first to smell the stream. Then, they all heard the tinkling and bubbling of fresh water rushing over rocks. It was like music to the creatures. Their pace was getting faster and faster as they got to the stream.

"Take it easy!" cried Mr. Gaster from inside the bottle.

"You will lose us if you are not careful."

But, from outside the bottle, all Tritus and Bufo could hear was the running water. As they approached the bank, the ground gave way to a more steep bank down to the water's edge. In his rush to get there faster, Tritus lost his grip on the bottle.

"Watch out, Bufo!" he shouted, but it was too late.

The bottle started to roll down the hill out of control, with Bufo hanging on for dear life. Mr. and Mrs. Gaster were desperately trying to keep some sort of balance in the bottle's water that was sloshing up and down and around them, but they were losing hope. Tritus and Arvi tried to catch up to the bottle, but Tritus tripped head over heels. Down they all rolled until *splash!* They all hit the water.

In the blink of an eye, the Gasters were out of the bottle and into the stream.

"Hooray, hooray!" they shouted.

Bufo popped up to the surface and was nearly hit by Tritus as he fell head-first into the stream. Then came Arvi with Rana on her shoulders, slipping gracefully into the water as only a water vole could.

"Ha ha! Hooray!"

Everyone laughed and splashed as they floated down the stream in a beautiful gurgle of fresh, clean water. Eventually, they came to some rocks next to a clump of tall bulrushes where they decided to rest.

"Well, I am glad we found this place," said Arvi.

"I think Bufo found it first!" laughed Rana.

Bufo rolled his eyes and made a circular motion with his head, and they all burst out in laughter again.

"Jolly good," smiled Tritus.

The group of friends spent the next two days and nights at the stream, exploring and feeding in the cool, clear water. Rana's leg was feeling much better. "I'm a quick healer," he would say with bravery as he showed his scar to everyone.

Mr. Gaster was back to his old self, with his glistening red throat and bright blue eyes. Mrs. Gaster also looked better than she had in a long while.

On the third day, they all could smell the rain coming. Arvi decided it was time to move on.

"It's just so lovely here," said Mrs. Gaster sadly.

"Yes, we really would love to stay here, Arvi," added Mr. Gaster.

"I know this, but remember what Erin said- when the rain comes, the stream will run much faster- so fast, that even sticklebacks will be washed away," Arvi reminded them.

Reluctantly, the Gasters returned to their bottle for traveling and the rest of the group began to haul them back up the bank. They made it to the top just in time as the rain started. Soon, the rain was coming down in giant drops and the trickle of the stream turned into a roar.

"Erin was not only kind, she was smart, too," noted Rana as a raindrop fell onto his head.

"Yes, you are right. Erin is smart," nodded Arvi.

"Is everybody ready? This is the way!" Rana called to the friends as he turned towards the large pasture.

"Right again," smiled Arvi.

Rana hopped over a large rock and touched his heels together in mid-air.

"Jolly good!" Tritus grinned.

"Why does he do that?" asked Bufo.

"Because, I can!" shouted Rana over his shoulder.

Chapter 6

Journey's End

"We must travel night and day now! Rest while we can," Arvi told the group of friends. Together, they made their way through the sedge grasses, coming across dandelions, buttercups, and daisies that looked just like bright yellow stars in a dark green night sky.

The next morning, the rain had stopped and the sun was out.

"It is warm today," noticed Rana, who was taking his turn rolling the Gasters' bottle with Arvi.

"Yes, I hope we find some water soon," agreed Tritus.

"A drop of rain would be welcome again," Bufo nodded.

But, rain did not come for many days and nights as they made their way through the hot, endless pasture. After what felt like forever to the creatures, Arvi called for a halt. They all moved under the shade of a large thistle. They were thirsty, hungry, and tired; the group of friends had come a very long way.

"The ground is too hard to dig for worms," groaned Bufo.

"Hey everyone, I don't think the Gasters are looking too well," Rana called as he peered into the bottle. Mrs. Gaster was floating on her back, gasping for breath, and Mr. Gaster had lost the bright red coloring to his throat.

"They need fresh water immediately," Arvi stated.

"We all do," replied Tritus.

"I must go and check the route ahead, wait here until I return," said Arvi as she bounded off past a large clump of daisies.

By the time she returned, all of the creatures were asleep under the shade of the thistle. She did not want to wake them. Quietly taking a closer look at the Gasters, she noticed they were both floating on their backs now, and their breathing was becoming shallow. Arvi knew they did not have much time before they needed to be in fresh water, but she was so tired, all she could do was curl up under the thistle with her friends and fall into a deep sleep throughout the dry, hot night.

It was Bufo who woke Arvi up in the morning.

"Arvi, Arvi!"

"What is it?" Arvi got up.

"It's the Gasters! They've gone! Disappeared! Bottle and all!" cried Bufo.

"What?! What could have happened to them?" asked Tritus.

"I can't believe that we have come all this way just to lose the Gasters!" Rana began to cry.

The group looked at each other, feeling defeated and upset about the sudden loss of their friends, the Gasters. It felt like the end.

"Dear, oh dear, what are we to do now?" Tritus looked to Arvi.

"We must carry on," said Arvi, "we must be brave and strong. There is nothing more we can do for the Gasters, but we must keep going."

"Yes, we have come this far, we should not give in now," agreed Rana.

"The Gasters would want us to go on," said Tritus.

"I agree," added Bufo, "we must go on."

So, Arvi, Tritus, Bufo, and Rana continued their journey together through the pasture. For three more days and nights without rain they carried on, weak with hunger, tired, hot, and thirsty, deep in their own thoughts about their lost friends, the Gasters.

On the fourth morning after the mysterious disappearance of the Gasters in their bottle, the creatures finally came to the end of the pasture. The ground was still too hard to dig through for precious worms since there had been no rain, and the group of friends were exhausted after their long journey. As they rounded a tall pile of rocks, they saw the shape of a large building in the distance.

"What on earth is that?" croaked a very weary Rana.

"It is the home of some Giant Feet," answered Arvi.

"Why have you brought us here, Arvi?" asked Bufo, confused.

"Yes, this is terrible! Are we lost?" Tritus cried out.

"I thought that we went on this long journey to get away from the Giant Feet!" Rana added.

"Everyone, listen to me," said Arvi calmly, "Tritus, can you smell the water?"

"Oh, uh, yes, I guess I can," replied Tritus, sniffing the air.

"Bufo, can you see the dragonflies?"

"Oh yes, I can see them," Bufo answered.

"And, Rana, do you think that I would lead all of my friends to this place if I thought it was filled with danger?"

Rana looked at Arvi.

"No," he admitted, "you are wise, and we trust you."

"Then follow me now. We are very close to the end of our journey," Arvi confidently stated.

The group made their way up a small hill of short cropped grass. When they reached the top of the hill, Arvi turned to her friends.

"Here we are, this is our new home!"

They all stared in wonder at the sight Arvi was pointing out. In front of them was a very large and beautiful Pond filled with lilies and bulrushes. A small, clear stream flowed out next to a group of willow trees. There were too many colorful wildflowers to count, and the air was full of the sounds of birds singing, bees buzzing, along with the dragonflies and damselflies.

"But- but- how? Why?" stammered a puzzled Rana.

"It was all built by the Giant Feet," answered Arvi.

"Is this a dream?" asked Bufo.

"Well, if it is, it's a jolly good one!" remarked an excited Tritus.

"Look!" shouted Rana, as he pointed out that there, in the shallows of this new Pond, was the unmistakable shape of the Gaster's bottle.

"How is this even possible?" the group asked Arvi.

"The Night Shadow," smiled Arvi.

"Night Shadow!" cried Rana, Tritus, and Bufo together.

"Yes, she has been guiding us all along. Remember your incident with the stoat creature, Rana? It was the Night Shadow who saved you. Remember that hot night we slept under the thistle in the pasture? It was the Night Shadow who took the Gasters in their bottle to this place."

The creatures shook their heads in wonder and disbelief. They did not know whether to laugh or cry, so they did both as they made their way to the beautiful new Pond to find the Gasters and explore their new home.

Chapter 7

Rana

It was a calm autumn evening and the sun was low on the horizon. Rana was sitting still in his new favorite spot. As he gazed over his new Pond, he thought about all of his friends. Mrs. Gaster had her many children, so the Pond was filled with young sticklebacks. Mr. Gaster was very proud and happy, of course anyone could tell by his glimmering bright red throat and his bright blue eyes. Arvi had built a new home on the far end of the Pond, Tritus was forever exploring the deeper waters, and old Bufo had found a new old log to crawl under. Rana had just met up with Tritus and Bufo the day before to talk about their journey together, and how happy they all were to be there.

Rana often thought of the Night Shadow, whom he had never met, and was thankful for the wise old tawny owl. He also thought of Erin the hedgehog, who had shown him kindness when he needed it the most after his encounter with the stoat creature. Rana thought of the Giant Feet, too: such strange creatures who seemed to have the power and right to destroy, yet the heart to be kind. Rana hoped that in the future, more Giant Feet would choose to create rather than destroy for the sake of all of the creatures.

Rana's thoughts soon turned to worms, of course, a feast of worms indeed. With that, he jumped very high and touched his heels together in mid-air, just because he could.

Lightning Source UK Ltd.
Milton Keynes UK
UKHW051925121022
410392UK00017B/103